EGLINTON INFANTS SCHOOL
PAGET RISE, SE18 3PY

A POT OF GOLD

Invitation

If you are a dreamer, come in,
If you are a dreamer, a wisher, a liar,
A hope-er, a pray-er, a magic bean buyer . . .
If you're a pretender, come sit by my fire
For we have some flax-golden tales to spin.
Come in!
Come in!

Shel Silverstein

A POT OF GOLD

A TREASURE TROVE OF POEMS

unearthed by Jill Bennett
all the colours of the rainbow
by Paddy Mounter

DOUBLEDAY

LONDON · NEW YORK · TORONTO · SYDNEY · AUCKLAND

For Audrey

TRANSWORLD PUBLISHERS LTD
61–63 Uxbridge Road, London W5 5SA

TRANSWORLD PUBLISHERS (AUSTRALIA) PTY LTD
15–23 Helles Avenue, Moorebank, NSW 2170

TRANSWORLD PUBLISHERS (NZ) LTD
Cnr Moselle and Waipareira Aves,
Henderson, Auckland

Doubleday Canada Ltd
105 Bond Street, Toronto, Ontario M5B 1Y3

Published 1989 by Doubleday Children's Books
a division of Transworld Publishers Ltd
Selection, arrangement and editorial matter
copyright © 1989 by Jill Bennett and Doubleday Children's Books
Illustrations copyright © 1989 by Paddy Mounter
British Library Cataloguing in Publication Data

A pot of gold
1. Children's poetry in English, 1945–   – Anthologies
I. Bennett, Jill (Jill Rosemary)
II. Mounter, Paddy
821'.914'0809282

ISBN 0 385 269692

Photoset by Rowland Phototypesetting Ltd
Bury St Edmunds, Suffolk
Printed in Portugal by
Printer Portugesa

Contents

Pearls

Emeralds

Diamonds

Tiptoe

Yesterday I skipped all day,
The day before I ran,
Today I'm going to tiptoe
Everywhere I can.
I'll tiptoe down the stairway.
I'll tiptoe through the door.
I'll tiptoe to the living room
And give an awful roar
And my father, who is reading,
Will jump up from his chair
And mumble something silly like
'I didn't see you there.'
I'll tiptoe to my mother
And give a little cough
And when she spins to see me
Why, I'll softly tiptoe off.
I'll tiptoe through the meadows,
Over hills and yellow sands
And when my toes get tired
Then I'll tiptoe on my hands.

Karla Kuskin

Where?

Where is that little pond I wish for?
Where are those little fish to fish for?

Where is my little rod for catching?
Where are the bites that I'll be scratching?

Where is the line for which I'm looking?
Where are those handy hooks for hooking?

Where is my rusty reel for reeling?
Where is my trusty creel for creeling?

Where is the worm I'll have to dig for?
Where are the boots that I'm too big for?

Where is there *any* boat for rowing?
Where is . . .
            Well, anyway, it's snowing.

David McCord

January

The days are short,
  The sun a spark
Hung thin between
  The dark and dark.

Fat snowy footsteps
  Track the floor.
Milk bottles burst
  Outside the door.

The river is
  A frozen place
Held still beneath
  The trees of lace.

The sky is low.
  The wind is gray.
The radiator
  Purrs all day.

John Updike

December Leaves

The fallen leaves are cornflakes
That fill the lawn's wide dish,
And night and noon
The wind's a spoon
That stirs them with a swish,

The sky's a silver sifter
A-sifting white and slow,
That gently shakes
On crisp brown flakes
The sugar known as snow.

Kaye Starbird

Tall Nettles

Tall nettles cover up, as they have done
These many springs, the rusty harrow, the plough
Long worn out, and the roller made of stone:
Only the elm butt tops the nettles now.

This corner of the farmyard I like most:
As well as any bloom upon a flower
I like the dust on the nettles, never lost
Except to prove the sweetness of a shower.

Edward Thomas

The Runaway

Once, when the snow of the year was beginning
  to fall,
We stopped by a mountain pasture to say,
  'Whose colt?'
A little Morgan had one forefoot on the wall,
The other curled at his breast. He dipped his
  head
And snorted to us. And then he had to bolt.
We heard the miniature thunder where he fled
And we heard him or thought we saw him dim
  and gray,
Like a shadow against the curtain of falling
  flakes.
'I think the little fellow's afraid of the snow.
He isn't winter-broken. It isn't play
With the little fellow at all. He's running away.
I doubt if even his mother could tell him, "Sakes,
It's only weather." He'd think she didn't know!
Where is his mother? He can't be out alone.'
And now he comes again with a clatter of stone,
And mounts the wall again with whited eyes
And all his tail that isn't hair up straight.
He shudders his coat as if to throw off flies.
'Whoever it is that leaves him out so late,
When other creatures have gone to stall and bin,
Ought to be told to come and take him in.'

Robert Frost

Giant Winter

Giant Winter preys on the earth,
Gripping with talons of ice,
Squeezing, seeking a submission,
Tightening his grip like a vice.

Starved of sunlight shivering trees
Are bent by his torturing breath.
The seeds burrow into the soil
Preparing to fight to the death.

Giant Winter sneers at their struggles,
Blows blizzards from his frozen jaws,
Ripples cold muscles of iron,
Clenches tighter his icicle claws.

Just as he seems to be winning,
Strength suddenly ebbs from his veins.
He releases his hold and collapses.
Giant Spring gently takes up the reins.

Snarling, bitter with resentment,
Winter crawls to his polar den,
Where he watches and waits till it's time
To renew the battle again.

John Foster

Hide and Seek

The trees are tall, but the moon small,
My legs feel rather weak,
For Avis, Mavis and Tom Clarke
Are hiding somewhere in the dark
And it's my turn to seek.

Suppose they lay a trap and play
A trick to frighten me?
Suppose they plan to disappear
And leave me here, half-dead with fear,
Groping from tree to tree?

Alone, along, all on my own
And then perhaps to find
Not Avis, Mavis and young Tom
But monsters to run shrieking from,
Mad monsters of no kind?

Robert Graves

The Paint Box

'Cobalt and umber and ultramarine,
Ivory black and emerald green –
What shall I paint to give pleasure to you?'
'Paint for me somebody utterly new.'

'I have painted you tigers in crimson and white.'
'The colours were good and you painted aright.'
'I have painted the cook and a camel in blue.
And a panther in purple.' 'You painted them true.

Now mix me a colour that nobody knows,
And paint me a country where nobody goes,
And put in it people a little like you,
Watching a unicorn drinking the dew.'

                                    E. V. Rieu

Jamaica Market

Honey, pepper, leaf-green limes,
Pagan fruit whose names are rhymes.
Mangoes, breadfruit, ginger-roots,
Granadillas, bamboo-shoots,
Cho-cho, ackees, tangerines,
Lemons, purple Congo-beans,
Sugar, okras, kola-nuts,
Citrons, hairy coconuts,
Fish, tobacco, native hats,
Gold bananas, woven mats,
Plantains, wild-thyme, pallid leeks,
Pigeons with their scarlet beaks,
Oranges and saffron yams,
Baskets, ruby guava jams,
Turtles, goat-skins, cinnamon,
Allspice, conch-shells, golden rum.
Black skins, babel — and the sun
That burns all colours into one.

Agnes Maxwell-Hall

19

The Star in the Pail

I took the pail for water when the sun was high
And I left it in the shadow of the barn nearby.

When evening slippered over like the moth's brown wing,
I went to fetch the water from the cool wellspring.

The night was clear and warm and wide, and I alone
Was walking by the light of stars as thickly sown

As wheat across the prairie, or the first fall flakes,
Or spray upon the lawn – the kind the sprinkler makes.

But every star was far away as far can be,
With all the starry silence sliding over me.

And every time I stopped I set the pail down slow,
For when I stooped to pick the handle up to go

Of all the stars in heaven there was one to spare,
And he silvered in the water and I left him there.

David McCord

The Woman of Water

There once was a woman of water
Refused a Wizard her hand.
So he took the tears of a statue
And the weight from a grain of sand
And he squeezed the sap from a comet
And the height from a cypress tree
And he drained the dark from midnight
And he charmed the brains from a bee
And he soured the mixture with thunder
And he stirred it with ice from hell
And the woman of water drank it down
And she changed into a well.

There once was a woman of water
Who was changed into a well
And the well smiled up at the Wizard
And down down that old Wizard fell . . .

Adrian Mitchell

21

Still the Dark Forest

Still the dark forest, quiet the deep,
Softly the clock ticks, baby must sleep!
The pole star is shining, bright the Great Bear,
Orion is watching, high up in the air.

Reindeer are coming to drive you away
Over the snow on an ebony sleigh,
Over the mountain and over the sea
You shall go happy and handsome and free.

Over the green grass pastures there
You shall go hunting the beautiful deer,
You shall pick flowers, the white and the blue,
Shepherds shall flute their sweetest for you.

And in the castle tower above,
The princess' cheeks burn red for your love,
You shall be king and queen of the land,
Happy for ever, hand in hand.

W. H. Auden

Hide and Seek

Call out. Call loud: 'I'm ready! Come and find me!'
The sacks in the toolshed smell like the seaside.
They'll never find you in this salty dark,
But be careful that your feet aren't sticking out.
Wiser not to risk another shout.
The floor is cold. They'll probably be searching
The bushes near the swing. Whatever happens
You mustn't sneeze when they come prowling in.
And here they are, whispering at the door;
You've never heard them sound so hushed before.
Don't breathe. Don't move. Stay dumb. Hide in your blindness.
They're moving closer, someone stumbles, mutters;
Their words and laughter scuffle, and they're gone.
But don't come out just yet; they'll try the lane
And then the greenhouse and back here again.
They must be thinking that you're very clever,
Getting more puzzled as they search all over.
It seems a long time since they went away.
Your legs are stiff, the cold bites through your coat;
The dark damp smell of sand moves in your throat.
It's time to let them know that you're the winner.
Push off the sacks. Uncurl and stretch. That's better!
Out of the shed to call to them: 'I've won!
Here I am! Come and own up I've caught you!'
The darkening garden watches. Nothing stirs.
The bushes hold their breath; the sun is gone.
Yes, here you are. But where are they who sought you?

Vernon Scannell

from **The Brook**

I slip,
   I slide,
      I gloom,
         I glance,

   Among my skimming swallows;
I make the netted sunbeams dance
   Against my sandy shallows.

I murmur under moon and stars
   In brambly wildernesses;
I linger by my shingly bars;
   I loiter round my cresses;

And out again I curve and flow
   To join the brimming river,
For men may come and men may go,
   But I go on forever.

        Alfred Lord Tennyson

Nuggets

A Word is Dead

A word is dead
When it is said,
Some say.
I say it just
Begins to live
That day.

Emily Dickinson

from Hullabaloo!

Hullabaloo!
The sun is high,
The clouds are whooshing across the sky,
Birds are soaring and winds are free,
Trees are tossing and we are WE!
(Nobody else we would rather be!)
Hullabalay baloo!

Barbara Willard

Sunflakes

If sunlight fell like snowflakes,
gleaming yellow and so bright,
we could build a sunman,
we could have a sunball fight,
we could watch the sunflakes
drifting in the sky.
We could go sleighing
in the middle of July
through sundrifts and sunbanks,
we could ride a sunmobile,
and we could touch sunflakes –
I wonder how they'd feel.

Frank Asch

The Crocus

The golden crocus reaches up
To catch a sunbeam in her cup.

Walter Crane

Mouth Open,
Story Jump Out

Mouth open
story jump out

I tell you me secret
you let it out

Besides,
the secret I tell you
wasn't even true
so you can shout
till you blue

So boo
mouth open
story jump out

But I don't care
if the world hear
shout it out

Mouth open
story jump out

John Agard

Bilberries

on the hillside
in shaggy coats
hobgoblin fruit
easy for little
hands

Gerda Mayer

The Bird's Nest

I know a place, in the ivy on a tree,
Where a bird's nest is, and the eggs are three,
And the bird is brown, and the eggs are blue,
And the twigs are old, but the moss is new,
And I go quite near, though I think I should have heard
The sound of me watching, if I had been a bird.

John Drinkwater

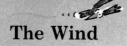

The Wind

I can get through a doorway without any key,
And strip the leaves from the great oak tree.
I can drive storm-clouds and shake tall towers,
Or steal through a garden and not wake the flowers.
Seas I can move and ships I can sink;
I can carry a house-top or the scent of a pink.
When I am angry I can rave and riot;
And when I am spent, I lie quiet as quiet.

James Reeves

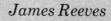

The Wind

The wind stood up and gave a shout;
He whistled on his fingers, and

Kicked the withered leaves about,
And thumped the branches with his hand.

And said he'll kill, and kill, and kill;
And so he will! And so he will!

James Stephens

Someone I Like

Someone I like is far away,
I feel the silence everywhere.
I didn't know how much I'd care.
Someone I like is far away,
I feel the silence in the air,
I feel it, feel it
                    everywhere.

Charlotte Zolotow

People

Some people talk and talk
and never say a thing.
Some people look at you
and birds begin to sing.

Some people laugh and laugh
and yet you want to cry.
Some people touch your hand
and music fills the sky.

Charlotte Zolotow

Clock

This clock
Has stopped,
Some gear
Or spring
Gone wrong –
Too tight,
Or cracked,
Or choked
With dust;
A year
Has passed
Since last
It said
Ting ting
Or tick
Or tock.
Poor
Clock.

Valerie Worth

Autumn

Yellow the bracken,
    Golden the sheaves,
Rosy the apples,
    Crimson the leaves;
Mist on the hillside,
    Clouds grey and white.
Autumn, good morning!
    Summer, good night!

Florence Hoatson

Bananas in Pyjamas

Bananas,
In pyjamas,
Are coming down the stairs;
Bananas,
In pyjamas,
Are coming down in pairs;
Bananas,
In pyjamas,
Are chasing teddy bears –
'Cos on Tuesdays
They all try to
CATCH THEM UNAWARES.

Carey Blyton

Monday's Child

Monday's child is fairly tough,
Tuesday's child is tender enough,
Wednesday's child is good to fry,
Thursday's child is best in pie.
Friday's child makes good meat roll,
Saturday's child is casserole.
But the child that is born on the Sabbath day,
Is delicious when eaten in any way.

Catherine Storr

The Man That Had Little to Say

I met a man at one o'clock who said 'Hello'
   at two.
At three o'clock he looked at me and said,
   'How do you do?'
At ten-to-four he said 'Good-by' and started
   on his way.
I'm glad he came to see me but he hadn't
   much to say.

John Ciardi

The Ceiling

Suppose the Ceiling went Outside
And then caught Cold and Up and Died?
The only Thing we'd have for Proof
That he was Gone, would be the Roof;
I think it would be Most Revealing
To find out how the Ceiling's Feeling.

Theodore Roethke

34

from **The Lord of the Rings**

Three rings for the Elven-Kings under the sky,
   Seven for the Dwarf-lords in their halls of stone,
Nine for Mortal Men doomed to die,
   One for the Dark Lord on his dark throne
In the Land of Mordor where the Shadows lie.
   One Ring to rule them all, One Ring to find them,
   One Ring to bring them all and in the darkness bind them
In the Land of Mordor where the Shadows lie.

J. R. R. Tolkien

Lemons and Apples

One day I might feel
Mean,
And squinched up inside,
Like a mouth sucking on a
Lemon.

The next day I could
Feel
Whole and happy
And right,
Like an unbitten apple.

Mary Neville

35

February Twilight

I stood beside a hill
  Smooth with new-laid snow,
A single star looked out
  From the cold evening glow.

There was no other creature
  That saw what I could see –
I stood and watched the evening star
  As long as it watched me.

Sara Teasdale

The Park

I'm glad that I
   Live near a park

For in the winter
   After dark

The park lights shine
   As bright and still

As dandelions
   On a hill.

      James Tippett

from Near the Window Tree

Wordless words.
A tuneless tune.
Blow out the sun.
Draw down the shade.
Turn off the dog.
Snap on the stars.
Unwrap the moon.
Wish leafy, sleeping trees good night
And listen
To the day shut tight.

      Karla Kuskin

Out in the Dark and Daylight

Out in the dark and daylight,
under a cloud or tree,

Out in the park and play light,
out where the wind blows free,

Out in the March or May light
with shadows and stars to see,

Out in the dark and daylight . . .
that's where I like to be.

Aileen Fisher

Pearls

Brother

I had a little brother
And I brought him to my mother
And I said I want another
Little brother for a change.
But she said don't be a bother
So I took him to my father
And I said this little bother
Of a brother's very strange.

But he said one little brother
Is exactly like another
And every little brother
Misbehaves a bit he said.
So I took the little bother
From my mother and my father
And I put the little bother
Of a brother back to bed.

Mary Ann Hoberman

The Answers

'When did the world begin and how?'
I asked a lamb,
   a goat,
     a cow.
'What is it all about and why?'
I asked a hog as he went by.
'Where will the whole thing end and when?'
I asked a duck,
   a goose
     a hen:
And I copied all the answers too,
A quack
   a honk
     an oink
       a moo.

Robert Clairmont

Parrot

Sometimes I sit with both eyes closed,
But all the same, I've heard!
They're saying, 'He won't talk because
He is a *thinking* bird.'

I'm olive-green and sulky, and
The family say, 'Oh yes,
He's silent, but he's *listening*,
He *thinks* more than he *says*!

'He ponders on the things he hears,
Preferring not to chatter.'
– And this is true, but *why* it's true
Is quite another matter.

I'm working out some shocking things
In order to surprise them,
And when my thoughts are ready I'll
Certainly *not* disguise them!

I'll wait and see, and choose a time
When everyone is present,
And clear my throat and raise my beak
And give a squawk and start to speak
And go on for about a week
And it will not be pleasant!

Alan Brownjohn

The Tide Rises, The Tide Falls

The tide rises, the tide falls,
The twilight darkens, the curlew calls;
Along the sea-sands damp and brown
The traveller hastens towards the town,
    And the tide rises, the tide falls.

Darkness settles on roofs and walls,
But the sea, the sea in the darkness calls;
The little waves, with their soft, white hands,
Efface the footprints in the sands,
    And the tide rises, the tide falls.

The morning breaks; the steeds in their stalls
Stamp and neigh, as the hostler calls;
The day returns, but nevermore
Returns the traveller to the shore,
    And the tide rises, the tide falls.

Henry Wadsworth Longfellow

Silver

Slowly, silently, now the moon
Walks the night in her silver shoon;
This way, and that, she peers, and sees
Silver fruit upon silver trees;
One by one the casements catch
Her beams beneath the silvery thatch;
Couched in his kennel, like a log,
With paws of silver sleeps the dog;
From their shadowy cote the white breasts peep
Of doves in a silver-feathered sleep;
A harvest mouse goes scampering by,
With silver claws, and silver eye;
And moveless fish in the water gleam,
By silver reeds in a silver stream.

Walter de la Mare

Dreams

Hold fast to dreams
For if dreams die
Life is a broken-winged bird
That cannot fly.

Hold fast to dreams
For when dreams go
Life is a barren field
Frozen with snow.

Langston Hughes

Things Men Have Made

Things men have made with wakened hands, and put
   soft life into
are awake through the years with transferred touch, and go
   on glowing
for long years.
And for this reason, some old things are lovely
warm still with the life of forgotten men who made
   them.

D. H. Lawrence

45

'Mummy, Oh Mummy'

'Mummy, Oh Mummy, what's this pollution
That everyone's talking about?'
'Pollution's the mess that the country is in,
That we'd all be far better without.
It's factories belching their fumes in the air,
And the beaches all covered with tar,
Now throw all those sweet papers into the bushes
Before we get back in the car.'

'Mummy, Oh Mummy, who makes pollution,
And why don't they stop if it's bad?'
''Cos people like that just don't think about others,
They don't think at all, I might add.
They spray all the crops and they poison the flowers,
And wipe out the birds and the bees,
Now there's a good place we could dump that old mattress
Right out of sight in the trees.'

'Mummy, Oh Mummy, what's going to happen
If all the pollution goes on?'
'Well the world will end up like a second-hand junk-yard,
With all of its treasures quite gone.
The fields will be littered with plastics and tins,
The streams will be covered with foam,
Now throw those two pop bottles over the hedge,
Save us from carting them home.'

'But Mummy, Oh Mummy, if I throw the bottles,
Won't that be polluting the wood?'
'Nonsense! that isn't the same thing at all,
You just shut up and be good.
If you're going to start getting silly ideas
I'm taking you home right away,
'Cos pollution is something that other folk do,
We're just enjoying our day.'

anon.

This is the Key

This is the key of the kingdom:
In that kingdom there is a city.
In that city there is a town.
In that town there is a street.
In that street there is a lane.
In that lane there is a yard.
In that yard there is a house.
In that house there is a room.
In that room there is a bed.
On that bed there is a basket.
In that basket there are some flowers.

Flowers in a basket.
Basket on the bed.
Bed in the room.
Room in the house.
House in the yard.
Yard in the lane.
Lane in the street.
Street in the town.
Town in the city.
City in the kingdom.
Of the kingdom this is the key.

anon.

Amulet

Inside the wolf's fang, the mountain of heather.
Inside the mountain of heather, the wolf's fur.
Inside the wolf's fur, the ragged forest.
Inside the ragged forest, the wolf's foot.
Inside the wolf's foot, the stony horizon.
Inside the stony horizon, the wolf's tongue.
Inside the wolf's tongue, the doe's tears.
Inside the doe's tears, the frozen swamp.
Inside the frozen swamp, the wolf's blood.
Inside the wolf's blood, the snow wind.
Inside the snow wind, the wolf's eye.
Inside the wolf's eye, the North Star.
Inside the North Star, the wolf's fang.

Ted Hughes

Yoruba Poem

Enjoy the earth gently
Enjoy the earth gently
For if the earth is spoiled
It cannot be repaired
Enjoy the earth gently

anon.

Dream Variation

To fling my arms wide
In some place of the sun,
To whirl and to dance
Till the white day is done.
Then rest at cool evening
Beneath a tall tree
While night comes on gently,
  Dark like me –
That is my dream!

To fling my arms wide
In the face of the sun,
Dance! Whirl! Whirl!
Till the quick day is done.
Rest at pale evening . . .
A tall, slim tree . . .
Night coming tenderly
  Black like me.

Langston Hughes

Emeralds

An emerald is as green as grass

An emerald is as green as grass;
   A ruby red as blood;
A sapphire shines as blue as heaven;
   A flint lies in the mud.

A diamond is a brilliant stone,
   To catch the world's desire;
An opal holds a fiery spark;
   But a flint holds fire.

Christina Rossetti

An Alphabet of Questions

Have Angleworms attractive homes?
Do Bumblebees have brains?
Do Caterpillars carry combs?
Do Dodos dote on drains?
Can Eels elude electric earls?
Do Flatfish fish for flats?
Are Grigs agreeable to girls?
Do Hares have hunting hats?
Do ices make an Ibex ill?
Do Jackdaws jug their jam?
Do Kites kiss all the kids they kill?
Do Llamas live on lamb?
Will Moles molest a mounted mink?
Do Newts deny the news?
Are Oysters boisterous when they drink?
Do Parrots prowl in pews?
Do Quakers get their quills from quails?
Do Rabbits rob on roads?
Are Snakes supposed to sneer at snails?
Do Tortoises eat toads?
Can Unicorns perform on horns?
Do Vipers value veal?
Do Weasels weep when fast asleep?
Can Xylophagans squeal?
Do Yaks in packs invite attacks?
Are Zebras full of zeal?

Charles Edward Carryl

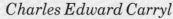

The Car Trip

Mum says:
'Right, you two,
this is a very long car journey.
I want you two to be good.
I'm driving and I can't drive properly
if you two are going mad in the back.
Do you understand?'

So we say,
'OK, Mum, OK. Don't worry,'
and off we go.

And we start The Moaning:
Can I have a drink?
I want some crisps.
Can I open my window?
He's got my book.
Get off me.
Ow, that's my ear!

And Mum tries to be exciting:
'Look out the window
there's a lamp-post.'

And we go on with The Moaning:
Can I have a sweet?
He's sitting on me.
Are we nearly there?

Don't scratch.
You never tell him off.
Now he's biting his nails.
I want a drink. I want a drink.

And Mum tries to be exciting again:
'Look out the window
There's a tree.'

And we go on:
My hands are sticky.
He's playing with the doorhandle now.
I feel sick.
Your nose is all runny.
Don't pull my hair.
He's punching me, Mum,
that's really dangerous, you know.
Mum, he's spitting.

And Mum says:
'Right I'm stopping the car.
I AM STOPPING THE CAR.'

She stops the car.

'Now, if you two don't stop it
I'm going to put you out the car
and leave you by the side of the road.'

He started it.
I didn't. He started it.

'I don't care who started it
I can't drive properly
if you two go mad in the back.
Do you understand?'

And we say:
OK, Mum, OK, don't worry.

Can I have a drink?

Michael Rosen

Cycling Down the Street to Meet my Friend John

On my bike and down our street,
Swinging round the bend,
Whizzing past the Library,
Going to meet my friend.

Silver flash of spinning spokes,
Whirr of oily chain,
Bump of tyre on railway line
Just before the train.

The road bends sharp at Pinfold Lane
Like a broken arm,
Brush the branches of the trees
Skirting Batty's Farm.

Tread and gasp and strain and bend
Climbing Gallows' Slope,
Flying down the other side
Like an antelope.

Swanking into Johnnie's street,
Cycling hands on hips,
Past O'Connors corner shop
That always smells of chips.

Bump the door of his back-yard
Where we always play,
Lean my bike and knock the door,
'Can John come out to play?'

Gareth Owen

Counting-out Rhymes

Hinty, minty, cuty, corn,
Apple seed, and apple thorn,
Wire, briar, limber lock,
Three geese in a flock.
One flew east, and one flew west,
One flew over the cuckoo's nest.
One two, three.
Out goes he.

anon.

One-ery, two-ery, zickery, seven;
Hollow bone, cracka bone, ten or eleven.
Spin, spun, it must be done,
Twiddledum, twaddledum, twenty-one.

anon.

Hoky, poky, winky, wum,
How do you like your taters done?
Snip, snap, snorum,
High populorum.
Kate go scratch it,
You are OUT.

anon.

Inty, minty, tibblety, fig,
Deema, dima, doma, dig;
Howchy, powchy, domi, nowchy,
Hom, tom, tout.
Olligo, bolligo, boo;
Out goes YOU.

anon.

Eenie meenie mackeracker
Air I dominacker
Chickie packer alleracker
Om pom push.
And O-U-T spells out.

John Wayne went to Spain
On a chocolate aeroplane,
Saw a ghost, eating toast
Halfway up a lamp-post,
And O-U-T spells out.

Inky Pinky Ponky
Daddy bought a donkey
Donkey died
Daddy cried
Inky Pinky Ponky.

anon.

Crawler

Creepy crawlers
creepy crawlers
creepy crawlers clutchers

terrible feelers
horrible touchers

creeping in your hair
crawling on your skin
nobody knows
how they get in

creeping from the north
crawling from the south
creeping down your forehead
crawling in your mouth

creeping on your tongue
crawling down your throat
into your gizzard
where they float float float.

Eve Merriam

Pedro

Pedro, the ice cream man,
Drives down our street
In his ice cream van.
And he brings:
      Barmybananapeanutcrunch
      Colaquenchandchococream
      Orangecoolermintymunch
      Ninetyninesandpineappledream.

Pedro, the ice cream seller,
Works every night
For his friend, Bertorella.
And he cooks:
      Hamburgersandhotdogs
      Freshfriedfishandjuicysteaks
      Jamdoughnutsandapplepie
      Sugaredwaffleshotpancakes.

Jennifer and Graeme Curry

The Serpent

There was a Serpent who had to sing.
There was. There was.
He simply gave up Serpenting.
Because. Because.
He didn't like his Kind of Life;
He couldn't find a proper Wife;
He was a Serpent with a soul;
He got no Pleasure down his Hole.
And so, of course, he had to Sing,
And Sing he did, like Anything!
The Birds, they were, they were Astounded;
And various Measures Propounded
To stop the Serpent's Awful Racket:
They bought a Drum. He wouldn't Whack it.
They sent – you always send – to Cuba
And got a Most Commodious Tuba;
They got a Horn, they got a Flute,
But Nothing would suit.
He said, 'Look Birds, all this is futile:
I do *not* like to Bang or Tootle.'
And then he cut loose with a Horrible Note
That practically split the Top of his Throat.
'You see,' he said, with a Serpent's Leer,
'I'm Serious about my Singing Career!'
And the Woods Resounded with many a Shriek
As the Birds flew off to the End of Next Week.

Theodore Roethke

It Makes a Change

There's nothing makes a Greenland Whale
Feel half so high-and-mighty,
As sitting on a mantelpiece
In Aunty Mabel's nighty.

It makes a change from Freezing Seas,
(Of which a Whale can tire),
To warm his weary tail at ease
Before an English fire.

For this delight he leaves the sea,
(Unknown to Aunty Mabel),
Returning only when the dawn
Lights up the breakfast table.

Mervyn Peake

What's Your Name?

What's your name?
Mary Jane.
Where do you live?
Cabbage Lane.
What's your number?
Rain and thunder.
What address?
Watercress.

What's your name?
Johnny Maclean.
Where do you live?
Down the lane.
What's your shop?
Lollipop.
What's your number?
Cucumber.

anon.

Step on a Crack

Step on a crack,
You'll break your mother's back;
Step on a line,
You'll break your father's spine.

Step in a ditch,
Your mother's nose will itch;
Step in the dirt,
You'll tear your father's shirt.

anon.

Imagine

Imagine a snail
As big as a whale,
Imagine a lark
As big as a shark,
Imagine a cat
As small as a gnat
And a bee as big as a tree.

Imagine a toad
As long as a road,
Imagine a hare
As big as a chair,
Imagine a goat
As long as a boat
And a flea the same size as me.

Roland Egan

Wishes

Said the first little chicken
With a queer little squirm,
'I wish I could find
A fat little worm.'

Said the second little chicken
With an odd little shrug,
'I wish I could find
A fat little slug.'

Said the third little chicken
With a sharp little squeal,
'I wish I could find
Some nice yellow meal!'

Said the fourth little chicken
With a small sigh of grief,
'I wish I could find
A little green leaf.'

Said the fifth little chicken
With a faint little moan,
'I wish I could find
A small gravel stone.'

'Now see here,' said their mother
From the green garden patch.
'If you want any breakfast,
Just come here and
　　　SCRATCH!'

anon.

The Muddy Puddle

I am sitting
In the middle
Of a rather Muddy
Puddle,
With my bottom
Full of bubbles
And my rubbers
Full of Mud,

While my jacket
And my sweater
Go on slowly
Getting wetter
As I very
Slowly settle
To the Bottom
Of the Mud.

And I find that
What a person
With a puddle
Round his middle
Thinks of mostly
In the muddle
Is the Muddi-
Ness of Mud.

Dennis Lee

The Witch's Cat

'My magic is dead,' said the witch. 'I'm astounded
That people can fly to the moon and around it.
It used to be mine and the cat's till they found it.
My broomstick is draughty, I snivel with cold
As I ride to the stars. I'm painfully old,
    And so is my cat;
    But planet-and-space-ship
    Rocket or race-ship
Never shall part me from that.'

She wrote an advertisement. 'Witch in a fix
Willing to part with the whole bag of tricks,
Going cheap at the price of eighteen and six.'
But no one was ready to empty his coffers
For out of date rubbish. There weren't any offers –
    Except for the cat.
    'But planet-and-space-ship
    Rocket or race-ship
Never shall part me from that.'

The tears trickled fast, not a sentence she spoke
As she stamped on her broom and the brittle stick broke,
And she dumped in a dustbin her hat and her cloak,
Then clean disappeared, leaving no prints;
And no one at all has set eyes on her since
    Or her tired old cat.
    'But planet-and-space-ship
    Rocket or race-ship
Never shall part me from that.'

Ian Serraillier

There Was a Young Lady of Riga

There was a young lady of Riga
Who went for a ride on a tiger:
    They returned from the ride
    With the lady inside
And a smile on the face of the tiger.

anon.

There Once Was a Barber of Kew

There once was a barber of Kew,
Who went very mad at the Zoo;
    He tried to enamel
    The face of a camel,
And gave the brown bear a shampoo.

Cosmo Monkhouse

The Old Fellow from Tyre

There was an old fellow of Tyre,
Who constantly sat on the fire.
    When asked, 'Are you hot?'
    He said, 'Certainly not.
I'm James Winterbotham, Esquire.'

anon.

The Walrus

The widdly, waddly walrus
has flippery, floppery feet.
He dives in the ocean for dinner
and stands on his noggin to eat.

The wrinkly, crinkly walrus
swims with a debonair splash.
His elegant tusks are of ivory
and he wears a fine walrus moustache.

The thundery, blundery walrus
has a rubbery, blubbery hide.
He puffs up his neck when it's bedtime
and floats fast asleep on the tide.

Jack Prelutsky

Mrs McPhee

Mrs McPhee
Who lived in South Zeal
Roasted a duckling
For every meal.

'Duckling for breakfast
And dinner and tea,
And duckling for supper,'
Said Mrs McPhee.

'It's sweeter than sugar,
It's clean as a nut,
I'm sure and I'm certain
It's good for me — BUT

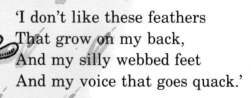

'I don't like these feathers
That grow on my back,
And my silly webbed feet
And my voice that goes quack.'

As easy and soft
As a ship to the sea,
As a duck to the water
Went Mrs McPhee.

'I think I'll go swim
In the river,' said she;
Said Mrs Mac, Mrs Quack,
Mrs McPhee.

Charles Causley

The Land of the Bumbley Boo

In the Land of the Bumbley Boo
The people are red white and blue,
They never blow noses,
Or ever wear closes,
What a sensible thing to do!

In the Land of the Bumbley Boo
You can buy Lemon pie at the Zoo;
They give away Foxes
In little Pink Boxes
And Bottles of Dandylion Stew.

In the Land of the Bumbley Boo
You never see a Gnu,
But thousands of cats
Wearing trousers and hats
Made of Pumpkins and Pelican Glue!

Chorus

Oh, the Bumbley Boo! the Bumbley Boo!
That's the place for me and you!
So hurry! Let's run!
The train leaves at one!
For the Land of the Bumbley Boo!
The wonderful Bumbley Boo-Boo-Boo!
The Wonderful Bumbley BOO!!!

Spike Milligan

72

Sir Nicketty Nox

Sir Nicketty Nox was an ancient knight,
So old was he that he'd lost his sight.
Blind as a mole, and slim as a fox,
And dry as a stick was Sir Nicketty Nox.

His sword and buckler were old and cracked,
So was his charger and that's a fact.
Thin as a rake from head to hocks,
Was this rickety nag of Sir Nicketty Nox.

A wife he had and daughters three,
And all were as old as old could be.
They mended the shirts and darned the socks
Of that old Antiquity, Nicketty Nox.

Sir Nicketty Nox would fly in a rage
If anyone tried to guess his age.
He'd mouth and mutter and tear his locks,
This very pernickety Nicketty Nox.

Hugh Chesterman

The Ship of Rio

There was a ship of Rio
   Sailed out into the blue,
And nine and ninety monkeys
   Were all her jovial crew.
From bo'sun to the cabin boy,
   From quarter to caboose,
There weren't a stitch of calico
   To breech 'em – tight or loose;
From spar to deck, from deck to keel,
   From barnacle to shroud,
There weren't one pair of reach-me-downs
   To all that jabbering crowd.
But wasn't it a gladsome sight,
   When roared the deep sea gales,
To see them reef her fore and aft
   A-swinging by their tails!
Oh, wasn't it a gladsome sight,
   When glassy calm did come,
To see them squatting tailor-wise
   Around a keg of rum!
Oh, wasn't it a gladsome sight,
   When in she sailed to land,
To see them all a-scampering skip
   For nuts across the sand!

Walter de la Mare

Buttons and Beads

There once was a woman
all buttons and beads
who made a good Seed Cake
without any seeds;

She made a rice pudding
without any rice –
she said, 'It's nutritious,
and really quite nice!'

She sewed up a jacket
without any sleeves,
she planted an oak tree
without any leaves;

And, one day, this woman
– why, what do you think? –
she filled up an ink well
without any ink!

She wrote a long letter
without any pen
and when she had finished
she started again.

Each night at her bed time
as likely as not
the hot tap ran cold
and the cold tap ran hot,

So she sewed them both up
without needle or thread,
and slept on the bath mat
without any bed!

Jean Kenward

The Sleepy Giant

My age is three hundred and seventy-two.
And I think, with the deepest regret,
How I used to pick up and voraciously chew
The dear little boys whom I met.
I've eaten them raw, in their holiday suits;
I've eaten them curried with rice;
I've eaten them baked, in their jackets and boots.
And I've found them exceedingly nice.

78

But now that my jaws are too weak for such fare,
I think it exceedingly rude
To do such a thing, when I'm quite well aware
Little boys do not like to be chewed.

And so I contentedly live upon eels,
And try to do nothing amiss.
And I pass all the time I can spare from my meals
In innocent slumber — like this.

Charles Edward Carryl

August Afternoon

Where shall we go?
　　What shall we play?
What shall we do
　　On a hot summer day?

We'll sit in the swing.
　　Go low. Go high.
And drink lemonade
　　Till the glass is dry.

One straw for you,
　　One straw for me,
In the cool green shade
　　Of the walnut tree.

Marion Edey

79

Hot Food

We sit down to eat
and the potato's a bit hot
so I only put a little bit on my fork
and I blow
whooph whooph
until it's cool
just cool
then into the mouth
nice.
And there's my brother
he's doing the same
whooph whooph
into the mouth
nice.
There's my mum
she's doing the same
whooph whooph
into the mouth
nice.
But my dad.
My dad.
What does he do?
He stuffs a great big chunk of potato
into his mouth.
Then
that really does it.

His eyes pop out
he flaps his hands
he blows, he puffs, he yells
he bobs his head up and down
he spits bits of potato
all over his plate
and he turns to us and he says,
'Watch out everybody –
the potato's very hot.'

Michael Rosen

Strange Service

A most peculiar postman
   is working down our street.
He doesn't *hand* the letters through –
   he does it with his feet.

A most unusual milkman
   is working in our town.
He swallows all the milk before
   he puts the bottles down.

A most uncommon dustman
   is working down our lane.
He takes the garbage round the back
   and throws it in again!

Kit Wright

Opals

Aiken Drum

There was a man lived in the moon
   and his name was Aiken Drum.
And he played upon a ladle,
   and his name was Aiken Drum.

And his hat was made of good cream cheese,
   and his name was Aiken Drum.
And he played upon a ladle, etc.

And his coat was made of good roast beef,
   and his name was Aiken Drum.

And his buttons were made of penny loaves,
   and his name was Aiken Drum.

His waistcoat was made of crust of pies,
   and his name was Aiken Drum.

His breeches were made of haggis bags,
   and his name was Aiken Drum.

anon.

My Uncle Paul of Pimlico

My Uncle Paul of Pimlico
Has seven cats as white as snow,
Who sit at his enormous feet
And watch him, as a special treat,
Play the piano upside-down,
In his delightful dressing gown;
The firelight leaps, the parlour glows,
And, while the music ebbs and flows,
They smile (while purring the refrains),
At little thoughts that cross their brains.

Mervyn Peake

The Stork

This is the tale of a poor old stork
Whose end was full of gloom;
For in a moment of carelessness
He went to meet his doom.

When poised in thought, one foot aloft,
While learning how to beg,
He went and quite forgot himself —
And raised the *other* leg.

Carey Blyton

Christmas Secrets

Secrets long and secrets wide,
brightly wrapped and tightly tied,

Secrets fat and secrets thin,
boxed and sealed and hidden in,

Some that rattle, some that squeak,
some that caution 'Do Not Peek' . . .

Hurry, Christmas, get here first,
get here fast . . . before we *burst*.

Aileen Fisher

A Perfect Pet

Now you have a papagouli
do be sure to treat it right –
he's a rather tender creature
and he doesn't like the light.

If you take him out in sunshine
that purple fur will fade,
and his tail will lose its curl
if you keep him in the shade.

He really can't see anything
unless the place is dark,
and if he doesn't see you
he will scrunch you like a shark.

Be sure he wears dark glasses
when you have to hit the trail –
take a really big umbrella
with an opening for his tail.

If he sneezes he gets savage,
ninety-nine things make him sneeze
and he's equally bad-tempered
if he's ruffled by the breeze.

A most demanding creature,
quite a problem, you can see –
now you have a papagouli
and my deepest sympathy.

Barbara Giles

87

The Gingerbread Lady

The gingerbread lady's
A bitter old maid, she's
Possessed of a terrible hunger.
She watches the girls
And the boys with crisp curls
Getting younger and younger and younger.

She pebbles her rooftop
With pastille and gob-stop
And gums by the dime and the dozen.
Smarties galore
Make a path to the door
Behind which she's stoking her oven.

Though her features are merry,
In desperate hurry
Her heart and her stomach are rumbling.
O alas and alack,
Down the dark forest track
You can hear the poor children come tumbling.

John Mole

It

It's orange and green and purple and pink,
It's covered with flowers and fruit,
A thing like a catapult hangs from one end,
The other end's shaped like a boot.
It wobbles, it waggles, it quivers and nods,
It rocks like a ship in a gale,
In sunlight it sparkles, in moonlight it glows,
In mist it resembles a whale.
It rustles, it whimpers, it sighs in the night,
It groans when you're trying to sleep,
It squats on the shelf like a being from space
Or a creature dredged up from the deep.
What is it – this monster, this madness, this mess,
This home for three mice and a bat,
This stranger amongst us, this guest in the house?
Don't touch it! It's Granny's new hat!

Richard Edwards

89

I Saw a Ship

I saw a ship a-sailing
A-sailing on the sea;
And, oh! it was all laden
With pretty things for me!

There were comfits in the cabin,
And apples in the hold;
The sails were made of silk,
And the masts were made of gold.

The four-and-twenty sailors
That stood between the decks,
Were four-and-twenty white mice
With chains about their necks.

The captain was a duck,
With a packet on his back;
And when the ship began to move,
The captain said, 'Quack! Quack!'

trad.

Owl of the Greenwood

'Owl
Who?
Who are you?
Who?'
    'I am owl,
      night's eyes,
      wise beyond understanding.'
'Who?
Who are you?
Who?'
    'I am owl,
      shadow of shadows,
      owner of forests,
      beautiful beyond comprehension.'
'Who?
Who are you?
Who?'
    'I am owl,
      plucker of moonbeams;
      owl, most mysterious.
      Beware.'

Patricia Hubbell

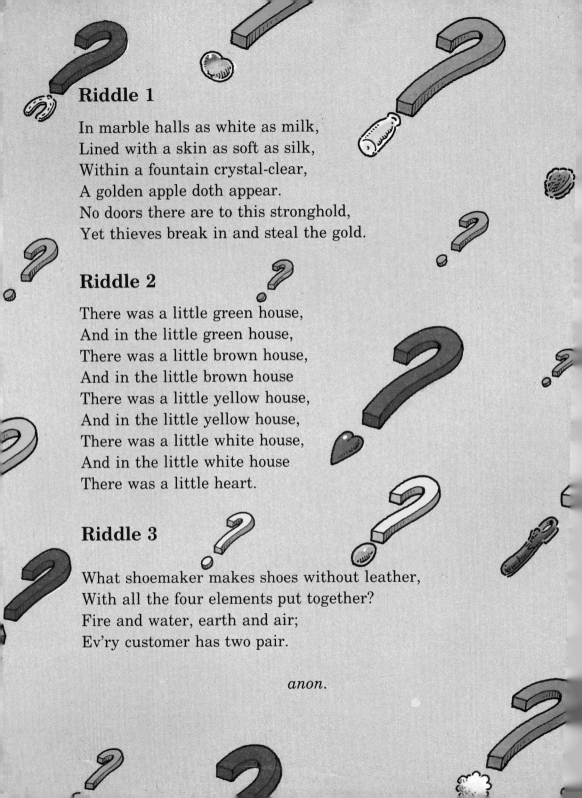

Riddle 1

In marble halls as white as milk,
Lined with a skin as soft as silk,
Within a fountain crystal-clear,
A golden apple doth appear.
No doors there are to this stronghold,
Yet thieves break in and steal the gold.

Riddle 2

There was a little green house,
And in the little green house,
There was a little brown house,
And in the little brown house
There was a little yellow house,
And in the little yellow house,
There was a little white house,
And in the little white house
There was a little heart.

Riddle 3

What shoemaker makes shoes without leather,
With all the four elements put together?
Fire and water, earth and air;
Ev'ry customer has two pair.

anon.

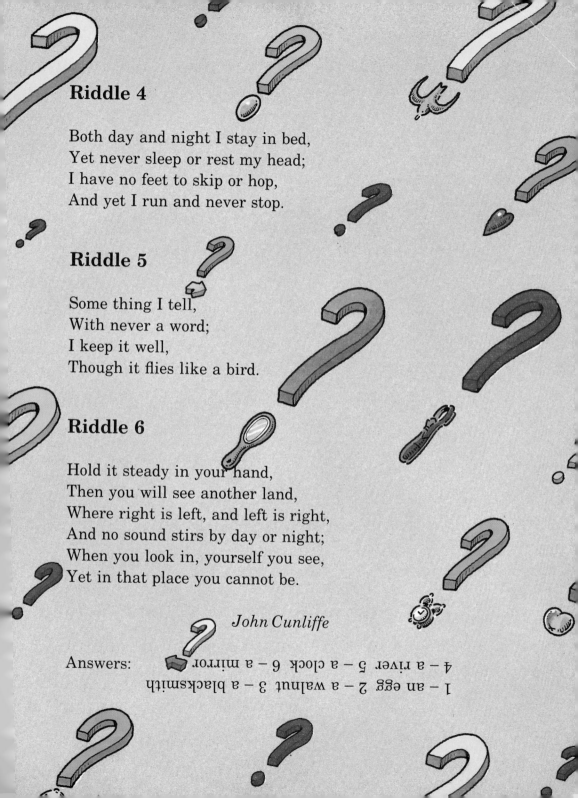

Riddle 4

Both day and night I stay in bed,
Yet never sleep or rest my head;
I have no feet to skip or hop,
And yet I run and never stop.

Riddle 5

Some thing I tell,
With never a word;
I keep it well,
Though it flies like a bird.

Riddle 6

Hold it steady in your hand,
Then you will see another land,
Where right is left, and left is right,
And no sound stirs by day or night;
When you look in, yourself you see,
Yet in that place you cannot be.

John Cunliffe

Answers: 1 – an egg 2 – a walnut 3 – a blacksmith 4 – a river 5 – a clock 6 – a mirror.

from **The King of China's Daughter**

The King of China's daughter,
So beautiful to see
With her face like yellow water
Left her nutmeg tree.
Her little rope for skipping
She kissed and gave it me
Made of painted notes of singing birds
Among the fields of tea.
I skipped across the nutmeg field
I skipped across the sea
And neither sun nor moon my dear
Has yet caught me.

Edith Sitwell

Micky Always

Bambalitty-Bambam,
Bambalitty-Bambam,
Everybody scram, scram.

Micky hit the ball so hard
it gone right out the yard
and break the lady window-pane.
He Micky don't hear, just don't hear.

Bambalitty-Bambam,
Bambalitty-Bambam,
Everybody scram, scram.

Micky break the lady window-pane
and when the lady come and complain
Mammy going give he plai plai
then you going hear Micky cry.

John Agard

Arvin Marvin Lillisbee Fitch

Arvin Marvin Lillisbee Fitch
Rode a broomstick like a witch.
Out of the window, over the trees,
Above the hills, across two seas,
And up and up on a wild moonbeam
Till he came to the other side of his dream,
Where he bumped his head a terrible thump
On top of the dark, and fell *ker-flump!* –
Down, down, down, down like a piece of lead,
Till he landed – *thud!* – in his very own bed.

He didn't cry. He didn't scream.
He simply said, 'When next I dream,
It seems to me it might be wise
To keep my dreams a smaller size.'

So saying, he went back to sleep
And dreamed about such things as sheep,
And birthday parties, and buttercups,
And toothpaste tubes, and spotted pups –
Good proper dreams, and none so tall
That he ran any risk of a fall.

Arvin's dreams were beautiful,
But perhaps a little dull.
In fact, but for the birthday cake
He might as well have stayed awake...
And in his sleep I heard him sigh,
'It was more fun when I dreamed high!'

John Ciardi

The Witch's House

Its wicked little windows leer
  Beneath a mouldy thatch,
And village children come and peer
  Before they lift the latch.

A one-eyed crow hops to the door,
  Fat spiders crowd the pane,
And dark herbs scattered on the floor
  Waft fragrance down the lane.

It sits so low, the little hutch,
  So secret, shy and squat,
As if in its mysterious clutch
  It nursed one knew not what

That beggars passing by the ditch
  Are haunted with desire
To force the door, and see the witch
  Vanish in flames of fire.

Laura Benét

Who's That?

Who's that
stopping at
my door in the
dark, deep
in the dead of the moonless night?

Who's
that in the quiet
blackness,
darker than dark?

Who
turns the han-
dle of my door, who
turns the old brass hand-
le of
my door with never a sound, the handle
that always
creaks and rattles and
squeaks but
now
turns
without a sound, slowly
slowly
      slowly
            round?

Who's that moving through the floor
as if it were a lake, an open door? Who
is it passes through
what can never be passed through,
who passes through
the rocking-chair
without rocking it,
who passes through
the table without knocking it, who
walks out of the cupboard without unlocking it?
Who's that? Who plays with my toys
with no noise, no
noise?

Who's that? Who is it
silent and silver
as things in mirrors, who's
as slow as feathers,
shy as the shivers,
light as a fly?

Who's that who's that
as close as
close as a hug, a kiss –

Who's THIS?

James Kirkup

The Hens

The night was coming very fast;
It reached the gate as I ran past.

The pigeons had gone to the tower of the church
And all the hens were on their perch,

Up in the barn, and I thought I heard
A piece of a little purring word.

I stopped inside, waiting and staying,
To try to hear what the hens were saying.

They were asking something, that was plain,
Asking it over and over again.

One of them moved and turned around,
Her feathers made a ruffled sound,

A ruffled sound, like a bushful of birds,
And she said her little asking words.

She pushed her head close into her wing,
But nothing answered anything.

Elizabeth Madox Roberts

from **The Witch's Work Song**

Two spoons of sherry
Three oz. of yeast,
Half a pound of unicorn,
And God bless the feast.
Shake them in the collander,
Bang them to a chop,
Simmer slightly, snip up nicely,
Jump, skip, hop.
Knit one, knot one, purl two together,
Pip one and pop one and pluck the secret feather.

T. H. White

The Mewlips

The shadows where the Mewlips dwell
　Are dark and wet as ink,
And slow and softly rings their bell,
　As in the slime you sink.

You sink into the slime, who dare
　To knock upon their door,
While down the grinning gargoyles stare
　And noisome waters pour.

Beside the rotting river-strand
　The drooping willows weep,
And gloomily the gorcrows stand
　Croaking in their sleep.

Over the Merlock Mountains a long and weary way,
　In a mouldy valley where the trees are grey,
By a dark pool's borders without wind or tide,
　Moonless and sunless, the Mewlips hide.

The cellars where the Mewlips sit
　Are deep and dank and cold
With single sickly candle lit;
　And there they count their gold.

Their walls are wet, their ceilings drip;
　Their feet upon the floor
Go softly with a squish-flap-flip,
　As they sidle to the door.

They peep out slyly; through a crack
   Their feeling fingers creep,
And when they've finished, in a sack
   Your bones they take to keep.

Beyond the Merlock Mountains, a long and lonely road,
   Through the spider-shadows and the marsh of Tode,
And through the wood of hanging trees and the gallows-weed,
   You go to find the Mewlips – and the Mewlips feed.

J. R. R. Tolkien

Jewels

In words, in books,
Jewels blaze and stream
Out of heaped chests
Or soft, spilled bags:
Diamonds, sharp stars,
Polished emerald tears,
Amethysts, rubies, opals
Spreading fire-surfaced pools,
Pearls falling down
In foam-ropes, sparks
Of topaz and sapphire strewn
Over a dark cave-floor –
How dim, then, the ring
Worn on the finger,
With one set stone.

Valerie Worth

What Happens to the Colors?

What happens to the colors
when night replaces day?
What turns the wrens to ravens,
the trees to shades of gray?

Who paints away the garden
when the sky's a sea of ink?
Who robs the sleeping flowers
of their purple and their pink?

What makes the midnight clover
quiver black upon the lawn?
What happens to the colors?
What brings them back at dawn?

Jack Prelutsky

Acknowledgements

Thanks are due to the copyright holders for permission to include the following material in this anthology.

John Agard, 'Mouth Open, Story Jump Out' from *Say It Again Granny*, by John Agard, and 'Micky Always' from *I Din Do Nuttin*, by John Agard, both illustrated by Susanna Gretz and reprinted by permission of The Bodley Head. **Anon**, 'Mummy, Oh Mummy', reprinted from *What On Earth*, ed. Judith Nicholls (Faber, 1989). **Frank Asch**, 'Sunflakes', reprinted from *Country Pie*, © 1979 by Frank Asch, by permission of Greenwillow Books (A Division of William Morrow and Company, Inc.). **W. H. Auden**, 'Still the Dark Forest', published in the UK in *The Ascent of F6* by W. H. Auden and Christopher Isherwood, and in the United States in *W. H. Auden: Collected Poems*, edited by Edward Mendelson, © 1976 by Edward Mendelson, William Meredith and Monroe K. Spears, Executors of the Estate of W. H. Auden. Reprinted by permission of Faber & Faber Ltd., and Random House Inc. **Laura Benét**, 'The Witch's House', reprinted from *Witch Words* (Faber & Faber Ltd.). **Carey Blyton**, 'Bananas in Pyjamas' and 'The Stork' from *Bananas in Pyjamas*, reprinted by permission of Carey Blyton, composer/author. **Alan Brownjohn**, 'Parrot' reprinted from *Brownjohn's Beasts*, by permission of the author. **Charles Causley**, 'Mrs McPhee' reprinted from *Early in the Morning* (Viking Kestrel) by permission of David Higham Associates Ltd. **Hugh Chesterman**, 'Sir Nicketty Nox', reprinted by permission of Basil Blackwell Ltd. **John Ciardi**, 'The Man That Had Little to Say' reprinted from *I Met a Man*, © 1961 by John Ciardi, by permission of Houghton Mifflin Company. 'Arvin Marvin Lillisbee Fitch' reprinted from *You Read to Me, I'll Read to You* (J. B. Lippincott), © 1962 by John Ciardi, by permission of Harper & Row, Publishers, Inc. **Robert Clairmont**, 'The Answers' from *For Me, Me, Me*, selected Dorothy Butler (Hodder & Stoughton Australia). **John Cunliffe**, 3 riddles from *Riddles, Rhymes and Rigmaroles* published by Andre Deutsch Ltd. Used by permission. **Jennifer & Graeme Curry**, 'Pedro' from *Down Our Street* (Methuen Children's Books). Used by permission. **Walter de la Mare**, 'Silver' and 'The Ship of Rio', reprinted by permission of The Society of Authors. **John Drinkwater**, 'The Bird's Nest' reprinted from *All About Me* copyright 1928 by John Drinkwater. Published by Houghton Mifflin Company. Used with permission. **Richard Edwards**, 'It' reprinted from *The Word Party*, by permission of Lutterworth Press. **Marion Edey**, 'August Afternoon' reprinted from *Open the Door* (New York: Scribner's, 1949), by permission of Charles

106

Index of Titles and First Lines

110

Last Song

To the Sun
Who has shone
   All day,
To the Moon
Who has gone
   Away,
To the milk-white,
Silk-white,
Lily-white Star
A fond goodnight
Wherever you are.

James Guthrie